Now Eye Can See

for Myself

A dad's personified reflection

W.O. Kitchen

To order additional copies of this book, contact:
Xlibris
844-714-8691
www.Xlibris.com
Orders@Xlibris.com

ISBN: Softcover   978-1-6641-8443-5
         EBook   978-1-6641-8442-8

Print information available on the last page

Rev. date: 08/20/2021

Now Eye Can See for Myself

I'm not going to the Doctor!

Doctors are no fun,

And doctors are not nice.

The last time we visited the Doctor,

That mean lady gave me a shot. Not once…But twice!

Daddy, you said, "it would only sting a little".

And that was not true,

You and Mommy both said, "I need to always be honest".

[Dad] Did I say that?

[Kamden] Yes. Daddy, it was you!

Daddy, I'm not coughing, and my tummy doesn't ache.

I don't want to go to the doctor.

I know…

You go! And I'll stay.

Kamden was so clever,
His dad smiled and tucked away a grin.
This smart and witty little boy,
Reminded him of him.

Kamden was wise beyond his years,
And smarter than Mommy and Daddy,
At least he'd supposed,
Well, I'll spill my drink all over my nice shirt,
Surely, there's no way I can go to the doctor with dirty clothes.

Mommy, now do I still have to go to the doctor?
Why, of course you do, Mommy said,
I'm disappointed that you've spilled your drink,
Let's get you another shirt instead.

So off to the closet Mommy went,
To return with a towel in hand,
[Mommy] Let's clean you up, Little Mister,
Look at you! Your arms and lips are all red.

But Mommy I don't want to go to the doctor,
The doctor always takes too long.
I have an idea!

Now what?
If I behave in the car, on the way there,
May we please, turn around and go home?

"Of course, not", she said, as she unbuckled his seat.

I want you on your best behavior,

When we walk through this door,

Not one sound,

Not one peep.

But, Mommy…

No buts, C'mon Kamden let's go!

If you're a good boy while we're here,

[She checks her purse] We'll stop for an ice cream cone.

As they entered the doctor's office,

Kamden was nervous,

His tummy twitched,

Something seemed strange about this place,

Mom… Dad… Where are the other kids?

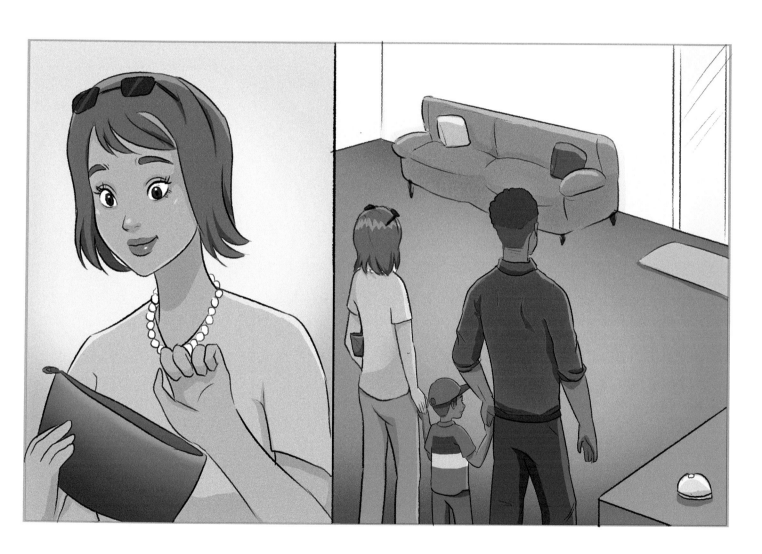

"Kamden"!

The nurse called, [as she grinned.]

Follow me Mom and Dad,

You too little fella,

Walk this way…

Go ahead. Walk right in.

Kamden held his daddy's hand,

As the family rounded the corner,

He whimpered again…

Almost sounding defeated…

But, I don't want to see the doctor…

You can sit in the "big boy seat",

Mom/Dad,

Do either of you care to hold him?

We're going to take some images of his eyes,

And it's very important that we keep his eyes opened.

So…

I'm not getting a shot?

No, Kamden that's what we've been trying to tell you.

Have a seat right here.

Now cover your left eye.

Can you see the numbers in green and yellow?

He nodded his head,
Which letters do you see?
He interrupted abruptly, "A", "Z", and "E",
Mom and Dad could clearly see the letters,
They were actually "A", "F", and "B".

The nurse scribbled on her notepad,

About what she observed.

Kamden, now excited was enjoying himself,

He thought they were spelling actual words.

But this chart was not for reading,

Or learning the alphabet,

The Snellen chart was not for spelling,

Or making words out of scrambled mess.

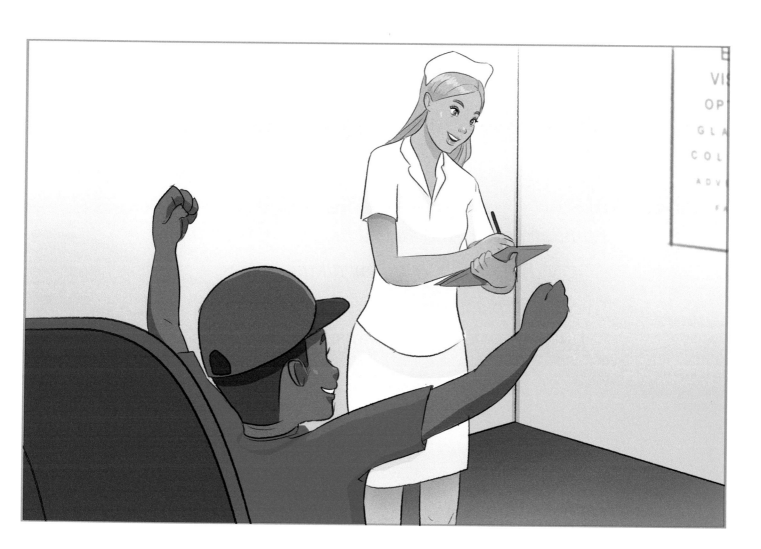

Kamden smiled and kicked his legs in excitement,
He thought he knew all the letters,
"Well, you're going to need glasses" the nurse said,
His mother said, "oh, you'll look so precious"!

Weak and strong eyes are examined,

With precision and delicate care,

Sometimes we must look beyond what we think we see,

And seek what's directly in front of us instead.

Our eyes control everything we see,

Thank God,

For His beauties to behold

Now Eye Can See what God intended me to see,

[Kamden] Are we still getting ice cream dad?

[Daddy smiled] Absolutely son. Let's go!

By,

W. O. Kitchen

Printed in the United States
by Baker & Taylor Publisher Services